J Mullar
Mullarkey, Lisa
Shakespeare saves the Globe /
$28.50

THE ART OF TIME TRAVEL

BARD OF AVON

SHAKESPEARE SAVES THE GLOBE

LONDON 1598 ENGLAND

∞ BY LISA AND JOHN MULLARKEY ∞
ILLUSTRATED BY COURTNEY BERNARD

Calico

An Imprint of Magic Wagon
www.abdopublishing.com

To Joanne Gordon: Thanks for sharing your
love of Shakespeare with Sarah.
—JM & LM

www.abdopublishing.com

Published by Magic Wagon, a division of ABDO, PO Box 398166, Minneapolis,
Minnesota 55439. Copyright © 2015 by Abdo Consulting Group, Inc.
International copyrights reserved in all countries. No part of this book may be
reproduced in any form without written permission from the publisher. Calico™
is a trademark and logo of Magic Wagon.

Printed in the United States of America, North Mankato, Minnesota.
102014
012015

 **THIS BOOK CONTAINS
RECYCLED MATERIALS**

Written by Lisa and John Mullarkey
Illustrated by Courtney Bernard
Edited by Tamara L. Britton and Bridget O'Brien
Cover and interior design by Candice Keimig

Library of Congress Cataloging-in-Publication Data

Mullarkey, Lisa, author.
  Shakespeare saves the Globe / by Lisa and John Mullarkey ; illustrated by
Courtney Bernard.
     pages cm. -- (The art of time travel)
  Summary: While helping to clean up their local community theater, twelve-
year-old Mason and his friend Aubrey suddenly find themselves in 1598 London
where a discouraged William Shakespeare has just lost his lease on the Globe and
is thinking about quitting writing--and it is up to the children to come up with a
plan to recover the theater and convince Shakespeare that the best is yet to come.
  ISBN 978-1-62402-090-2
1. Shakespeare, William, 1564-1616--Juvenile fiction. 2. Globe Theatre
(London, England : 1599-1644)--Juvenile fiction. 3. Time travel--Juvenile
fiction. 4. Dramatists, English--Early modern, 1500-1700--Juvenile fiction.
5. London (England)--History--16th century--Juvenile fiction. 6. Great Britain-
-History--Elizabeth, 1558-1603--Juvenile fiction. [1. Shakespeare, William,
1564-1616--Fiction. 2. Globe Theatre (London, England : 1599-1644)--Fiction.
3. Time travel--Fiction. 4. London (England)--History--16th century--Fiction.
5. Great Britain--History--Elizabeth, 1558-1603--Fiction.] I. Mullarkey, John,
author. II. Bernard, Courtney, illustrator. III. Title.
  PZ7.M91148Sh 2015
   813.6--dc23

                                        2014034365

TABLE of CONTENTS

Meet William Shakespeare

William Shakespeare is one of the greatest writers of all time. His use of poetry and prose to express deep feelings and thoughts is unsurpassed in literature.

Despite his fame, little is known about Shakespeare's life. However, we know that he was born in Stratford-upon-Avon, Warwickshire, England, in 1564. He was the third of John and Mary Shakespeare's eight children. The exact date of his birth is unknown, but he was baptized on April 26 of that year.

When he was 18 years old, Shakespeare married Anne Hathaway. They had three children. Their first child was a daughter they named Susanna. Later came twins, a son, Hamnet, and another daughter, Judith.

By 1592, Shakespeare was in London, working as an actor and playwright. He joined the acting group Lord Chamberlain's Men. The following year, a plague epidemic forced the closing of London's theaters. During this period, Shakespeare wrote his narrative poems and some early sonnets.

Until 1598, Shakespeare worked in two playhouses, the Theatre and the Curtain, that were managed by James Burbage. Burbage's son Richard was a famous actor and Shakespeare's friend. This same year, the Burbages, Shakespeare, and several others built the Globe Theatre. Shakespeare was associated with the Globe for the remainder of his career.

In 1610, William Shakespeare retired and returned to his hometown. He died there on April 23, 1616. During his career, he wrote 36 plays, 154 sonnets, and 2 narrative poems.

THE AUSTIN

"Want one, Mason?" asked Aubrey as she held out a tray of cookies. "I made them heart-shaped in honor of the big scene today."

The big scene was Romeo kissing Juliet during rehearsal. My mom was playing Juliet.

Aubrey plopped the tray down on a rickety table in the prop room and grabbed a broom.

"The red sprinkles taste like cinnamon," she said as she swept dust bunnies out of a corner. "Eat as many as you want. Just don't get crumbs on the floor or I'll have to sweep again."

Aubrey and I met a few summers ago here at the Austin Community Theater. It's a tiny theater in Austin, Texas. It's in an old historic brick building downtown. The building is pretty cool. A historic preservation group saved it from demolition. Everyone calls it the Austin.

Both of our moms are rehearsing for the annual summer play. This year, it's William Shakespeare's *Romeo and Juliet*. Aubrey comes to rehearsals because she wants to. I come because I have to. Even though I'm twelve years old, my mom thinks I'm still too young to stay home alone.

I swiped a cookie from the tray. Aubrey always brought desserts in for the cast and crew. If I had to spend four or five hours here every day over summer vacation, at least it was with someone who loved sugar as much as I did.

"My mom calls this theater her second home because she's here more than she's at our house," said Aubrey.

I scanned the area. "My mom should call this place a second home, too. Want to know why?"

"Because she's always here?" asked Aubrey.

I shook my head. "No, because half of this stuff

used to be in my house." I pointed to a coffee maker in the corner. "That stopped working last summer." Then I pointed out things that used to be ours: the green love seat, tattered luggage, a broken television, my dad's ten-speed bike, and a couple of lamps.

"I even found a box of Chinese checkers in the closet with Mason Mansfield written on it," I said. "I was surprised when I found it. I had tossed it in the box to be donated to Goodwill. My mom said it was used for a scene in the holiday play."

Aubrey laughed. "Most families recycle their junk. Apparently, your family sends it to the theater!"

She took window cleaner and sprayed a mirror. Aubrey was a neat freak. She hated dirt and was always worried about germs. She kept a tiny bottle of hand sanitizer in her pocket at all times.

"Since the kissing scene is today," said Aubrey. "I had to make heart-shaped something, ya know?"

"Did you see the sign on the dressing room door?" she asked. "It says, Pucker Up, Paul."

Paul was the actor who played Romeo. He was in college now but had started acting here when he was in third grade. He was about to kiss my mom for the first time.

"I saw it." I groaned. "Don't remind me." Picturing my mom kissing anyone but my dad was just wrong.

I had helped my mom study her lines all summer. I had them memorized before she did. "Did you make the sign?" I grabbed another cookie.

"Not me," she said as she pushed her glasses up the bridge of her nose. She handed me a napkin. "Paul laughed when he saw it and asked if anyone had lip gloss."

"I wish opening night was tonight," I said. "So then we wouldn't have to come to rehearsals anymore." I wiped my mouth, crumpled up the napkin, and tossed it into the trash can. "Did you know I was the only kid in my neighborhood that wasn't at the skate park yesterday? And all my friends are swimming at Barton Springs today. And where am I? Stuck here!"

She inspected the mirror. "You may not have to worry about it much longer. I overheard my mom talking to Miss Lucy this morning. She said this is the third play in a row that has had low ticket sales. If the theater doesn't start making money, it may have to close down."

"Don't worry," I said. "There are still two weeks left until opening night. Sales will pick up. But to be honest, I wouldn't mind if this place closes down. I hate coming here."

She threw the rag at me. "That's an awful thing to say, Mason. This theater makes a lot of people happy. If it closes, Miss Lucy would lose her job."

Now I felt bad. Miss Lucy let us sell tickets with her on opening night.

"If it weren't for the Austin, we wouldn't have met," said Aubrey. "Or any of the other kids. It would be sad if it closed." She blew dust off the frame of the mirror. "I wish rehearsals were twenty-four hours a day. I love it here."

I tried to cheer her up. "My mom says you shouldn't worry about things that may never happen."

She sighed. "My mom says the same thing." She closed her eyes. "Okay. I'm going to think positive." She opened her eyes and handed me another cookie. "Well? How are they?"

I stuffed it into my mouth. "I give these a nine. They're almost as good as your snickerdoodles." I plucked another cookie from the tray. "Almost."

Paul walked into the room and grabbed a sword from a box. He picked up a cookie and took a bite. He scrunched his nose. "I give it a five. Cinnamon isn't my thing."

"A five? A plague o' both your houses!"

Paul's eyes lit up. "Bravo! You probably know the whole play." He sliced his sword through the air. "I'm off to slay a foe and then kiss my Juliet."

Don't remind me. He left a trail of crumbs behind.

Aubrey followed with a broom and a dustpan to sweep them up. "I used a different shortening last night. They're crumbly." Then she got excited. "Wait until you see my cupcakes with green and blue frosting tomorrow. They look like globes."

"Globes?" I asked. "School doesn't start for another month."

She smirked. "School? Didn't I ever tell you about the new Globe Theatre?"

"Is that the new theater at the mall?" I asked.

Her ponytail swished from side to side. "Nope. Shakespeare's Globe is in London. It has a replica of the original Globe Theatre. My family went there on vacation over spring break. We saw *Romeo and Juliet*."

"What happened to the original Globe Theatre?" I asked.

"In 1613, during a performance of *Henry VIII* ..." She paused and bit her lip. "Maybe it was *Hamlet*? I'm not sure which one it was. But I'm positive it started with an *H*."

"Yeah, well what happened?" I asked again.

"They shot off a real cannon. It set the theater on

fire and it burned down. Back then, it had a thatch roof so . . . poof!"

"They actually used a real cannon?" I asked.

She nodded. "It reopened a year later but was shut down again by some religious group. Shakespeare wrote most of the plays that were performed there."

"I can't believe you saw a building from the seventeenth century."

"I didn't." She looked disappointed. "The theater was torn down eventually. But archaeologists uncovered its foundation around twenty-five years ago. After that, an exact replica was built near the original site. That's where we saw *Romeo and Juliet*."

"An exact replica?" I asked.

I nodded. "Except it has modern stuff like plumbing and electricity. When we saw the play, it was staged outside just like when Shakespeare was alive. We stood in the yard like the groundlings."

"Groundlings?" I asked. "They sound like a bunch of squirrels."

Aubrey pulled the plastic wrap over her cookies. "The groundlings were the commoners. They weren't rich but they weren't exactly poor. They paid a penny to see the play and had to stand the entire time. The tour guide told us it was a lot like sitting in the bleachers at a baseball game."

"So that's how you know so much about Shakespeare?" I said.

"Yep. Now that I've been to Shakespeare's Globe, I'm his number one fan."

"But he's so boring!" I argued.

Aubrey dropped the broom and dustpan. She fell to her knees and stretched out her arms toward me. "O Romeo, Romeo! Wherefore art thou Romeo?" She stood up. "Do you call that boring?"

"Very boring," I said.

"Maybe you're the boring one," she said as she looked at cast pictures on the wall. "I love the Austin. It gives me that cozy feeling." She stood up and started sweeping.

The Austin was cozy. Too cozy. The backstage area was crowded. When the actors waited in the wings, they had to stand with their backs against the walls so they didn't interfere with the action on stage. It smelled like old building and new paint.

Aubrey emptied the dustpan into the trash can. "I'm already starting to think of a cake I can make to celebrate its fiftieth anniversary next year."

If it makes it to fifty years, I thought. But I knew better than to say that.

The theater used to be a general store. The front door sits between two display windows. They are full of props that advertise the current play. Flyers announcing show times hang in the windows.

The building is long and narrow. When you enter the theater there is a short lobby. A table to the right is where Miss Lucy sells tickets. To the left is a table with a jar for donations and information on upcoming plays and community events.

Between the two tables, directly across from the

entrance door are double doors that lead inside. Rows of green seats that were salvaged from an old movie theater face the stage. There are 250 seats. I must have counted them at least a hundred times every summer. When I could have been outside having fun.

"My dad has a business trip to London next summer," said Aubrey. "Maybe you can come with us. We'll take you to the Globe Theatre."

I put my hands around my neck, stuck my tongue out, and pretended I was choking. "No thanks."

"Don't be a party pooper. Can you imagine what it was like at the original Globe Theatre? Maybe we could see a play."

I was tired of plays and being stuck inside while my friends were having fun outside. "No," I said as I pulled out a sword from a box and sliced through the air. "No more plays. I'd rather end it like Romeo than go to the Globe Theatre." I lifted the sword and pretended to pierce my heart. I sputtered, "Good-bye my Aubrey . . . till we meet again."

Aubrey clapped. "Not bad." She rummaged through a rack of costumes and stopped when she saw a gold satin dress. "This is beautiful, isn't it? I don't remember seeing it before." She slid the dress off of the hanger and held it up in front of the mirror. "I love the way it shimmers." She threw it on over her jeans and shirt and tied the sash in the back.

She squealed. "It fits! If I ever go back to the Globe Theatre, I'm going to wear it."

She spun in a circle. And as she did, a flash of light burst from the dress. It was so bright that I had to cover my eyes. Each time I tried to open them, I couldn't because a bunch of little flashes followed.

I don't remember much after that except Aubrey's panicky voice in my ear.

"Wake up, Mason. I don't think we're in Texas anymore."

WHERE ARE WE?

Aubrey shook my shoulder. "Are you okay?"

I was groggy. "Why do I feel like I just got off a roller coaster? My head's spinning." I groaned. "What just happened?"

Aubrey stood and looked around. "Where exactly are we? My glasses fogged up."

For a moment, her voice sounded like it was in a bottle. I had to shake my head several times before the muffled effect disappeared. I sat there a second to get my bearings before noticing the stench.

I sat up and quickly pinched my nostrils together. "What is that awful smell?"

Aubrey gagged and then pinched her nostrils, too. "We're in an alley." She pointed to a group of wooden barrels. "Where'd they come from?"

I stood and leaned against a wall. We seemed to be in a dark, cramped alley between two buildings. The ground was clammy and wet. Water dripped down onto us from somewhere up above. I moved toward the barrels and peeked inside. They were half-filled with a slimy, greenish-brown liquid. It smelled terrible!

I jumped back and slipped on the sludge leaking out of one of them.

Aubrey pulled me to my feet. "Look at all of this garbage! It's like someone came down here and threw away their trash. And apparently it's been going on for quite a while."

She surveyed the area. "There's chicken bones, egg shells, clam shells, rotten vegetables, and ..." Her face turned white. "I can't even guess what this gooey black stuff is."

"This is disgusting," I said. "We better go and tell Miss Lucy that someone's been dumping garbage outside the theater."

Aubrey's voice quivered. "Mason, this doesn't look like the Austin at all, does it?" Then she screamed. "Did you see that thing crawl behind the barrel? I think it was a . . ."

"Rat!" I yelled as I tried to jump out of the way.

It was too late. Three large black rats scurried between my feet and followed the other one behind the barrels.

Aubrey screamed again and pushed her back against the wall. I grabbed her hand and pulled her up the alley. We had to jump over piles of trash, wood, and bricks before we found a wider, brightly lit opening.

Please let that be a street, I thought.

As we got closer, the alley wasn't as cluttered with garbage. We stopped short of the opening to catch our breath and figure out just where we were. I was trying not to panic.

"Something's wrong," said Aubrey. "Really wrong. I just know it."

"Yeah. Not only is this smell unbearable, but things don't feel right. Maybe we're dreaming."

"A dream? This alley is a nightmare!" Aubrey said. "Did you see the size of those rats? I don't even want to know what was in those barrels." She pushed past me. "Let's get out of here."

As we got closer to the light, we heard the bustling sounds of a busy street. There were people laughing and yelling, dogs barking, and the clanking and hammering of tools.

"Do you hear chickens clucking?" asked Aubrey.

"I heard a horse," I said. "And dogs. If you listen carefully, you can hear cats fighting."

Aubrey still had her hand covering her nose. "I hear a bell. It sounds like a church bell."

My stomach dropped. We didn't have church bells that rang like that in Austin.

We took a few steps into the street and froze.

"Whoa," Aubrey said. "This isn't Austin. It doesn't look like any place I've ever been to in Texas, either."

I thought the same thing. "It doesn't even look like we're in the United States. There aren't any cars. No streetlights. There are animals everywhere." I pointed to the street. "It's not even paved."

We stood on a busy, narrow gravel street that had small stone sidewalks on both sides. There were dozens of tall white and black buildings and open-air shops and stores surrounding us. Many of the storefronts were decorated with holly and pine. It looked like Christmas. Piles of wood, rocks, and garbage littered the streets. It was a lot cooler than it was when I got dressed this morning. It wasn't exactly cold but it sure didn't feel like a July day.

People dressed in strange but colorful clothing walked along the street. Most of them were men and many had beards and mustaches. They wore hats, black knee-high boots, and long jackets. Some of the men wore fancy robes.

"I look a little out of place here in my shorts and sweatshirt," I said.

But the weird thing was that no one seemed to notice or care.

Many of the women looked like Aubrey in her dress except they were rounder and wore hats or bonnets decorated with jewels or feathers. One woman balanced a large basket of apples on her head as she dodged through the crowd.

"Did you notice how round everyone looks? The dresses are huge," said Aubrey. "They must have padding underneath."

In front of us, a horse-drawn wagon hauled large sacks. It struggled to get through the crowds of men who were pushing carts. The driver seemed angry and yelled. A small child picked up a rock and threw it at the man.

Shopkeepers and vendors shouted over each other.

"This is bedlam," said Aubrey. "Total chaos."

I was afraid to move or ask someone where we were or what was going on. "This is either great scenery for a play, or we went back in . . ."

"Time?" said Aubrey. "I was thinking the same thing but was afraid to say it. Is it even possible?" Her eyes watered. "I've read books about time travel but assumed it couldn't really happen."

Before I answered, a man carrying a sack over his shoulder brushed passed us and trudged into the same alley we had just come out of.

"Phew!" I said as he passed. "That guy needs a shower."

Aubrey's voice cracked. "Do you think he knows about the rats down there?"

A minute later, we got our answer. He came out of the alley dangling a squirmy rat in one hand and rotted vegetables in the other.

He licked his lips and spoke. "I got me a juicy one. My family will feast tonight."

As he walked away, the boy who threw the rock ran over to pet the rat.

Aubrey was horrified. "That is completely disgusting. Can you imagine the germs on that thing?"

I wasn't sure if she meant the juicy rat, the smelly man, or the filthy kid.

A woman approached us. "Don't waste your time in that alley there. If you're hungry, the theater will be open soon and you can scrounge around for some apples on the floor."

"The floor?" said Aubrey.

"Calm down," I whispered. I turned back to the lady. "Where's the theater?"

She pointed. "Twenty yards over there. For a penny, the Curtain will entertain you."

Aubrey looked confused. "The Curtain? I think I've heard of it before but I can't remember where." Her brow furrowed as she thought.

"In Texas?" I asked, crossing my fingers. I still hoped this was just a dream.

She shrugged. "We're about to find out."

We hurried along the sidewalk until it ended at a cobblestone court.

"This must be it," I said.

In front of us stood an unusual looking circular building with an arched entrance. It was painted white and had brown wooden beams holding up a thatched roof. There was a tall tower connected above the roof. Two flags, red and black, were resting on the bottom of a pole. But on the highest pole, a white flag waved proudly.

"This building looks like a stadium or an arena of some kind," I said.

"Look over there toward the back," said Aubrey. "There's a door with a sign above it." She shifted her feet and eyes. "I don't feel comfortable out here. Let's go over there and see if someone can help us."

We rushed over and read the wooden sign above the door. "Tiring room?" Aubrey said. "Do they replace tires in there?"

We poked our heads inside.

"No one's here," I said. "Let's go in."

Once inside, we felt better. There were a few candles lit and the room smelled of perfume.

"It smells a million times better in here than out there," said Aubrey. "It's a lot cleaner, too." She glanced around the room. "Except for the floor."

The wooden floor was covered in sawdust and there was a broom leaning on a chair. Aubrey grabbed it and started to sweep.

In the middle of the room, there were several large tables covered with rolls of fabric and spools of thick thread. On the far wall in between two doors, there was a fireplace with a clothesline across it.

"It looks like someone was drying clothes," I said.

Then I noticed two workbenches under the windows. Old tools were scattered on top of them. On the left side of the room, colorful dresses and jackets hung from a wooden rack. Above the clothes dozens of hats and wigs hung on pegs.

"Look at all this stuff," said Aubrey. "It reminds me of the prop room at the Austin." Then she slapped her forehead. "Mason, I bet tiring room is another name for prop room or dressing room. It has to be."

Leaning next to the fireplace were several swords, knives, and other weapons. A couple of the swords looked as though they were just painted and were drying. A bunch of old musical instruments hung on the wall above the mantle.

While we were looking at the swords, two men carried in a bunch of clothes. They piled them on one of the workbenches and left without saying anything to us. Then suddenly, the door to the right of the fireplace opened and a man hurried in. He was busy flipping through several sheets of paper. He walked over and stood by the window.

His forehead was high and he had a neatly trimmed beard and mustache. Longer reddish-brown hair reached down in the back to his collar. He wore a thick, padded brown vest over a shiny brown jacket. His belt held a silver dagger or small sword. I wondered if it were real.

He had a frilly white ruff around his neck and wore heavy velvet pants over dark stockings that came up to his knees. His shoes looked like slippers with buckles. He looked over and seemed agitated when he saw us.

"By stars, have you raised the black flag for today's performance yet? I have no idea why the white flag waves. This play is not a comedy."

Then upon closer inspection of us, he frowned. "And who might I ask are you both?"

"I'm Mason and this is my sister, Aubrey. We were just looking around."

Aubrey gave me a strange look.

He looked at Aubrey. "Women are not welcome in this room."

Aubrey clenched her hands and quickly scanned the area and pointed to the clothes on the workbench. "If I am not welcome, then I shall take all of the dresses I brought here with me back home."

The man looked surprised and swiped the hat off his head. "Forgive me, my lady! I did not know that this theater benefited from your generosity."

Aubrey was a good actress. By the look on her face, I knew she was impressed with herself, too.

"What play is being performed here?" she asked. "I would like to know where my good clothes have gone. I do hope it's a fine one."

"The play is indeed a fine one," said the man. "It is *Romeo and Juliet*."

Aubrey sucked in her breath. "*Romeo and Juliet*?"

Now it was my time to act. "Have you seen it?" I asked him. "How do you know it's a fine one?"

A smile slowly spread across the man's face.

"Because I wrote it. I am William Shakespeare."

Aubrey looked startled. She started to mumble something but her words weren't clear. As he leaned forward to figure out what she was trying to say, the door opened again.

"Robert!" said Shakespeare. "What brings you here?"

Aubrey turned to me and mouthed, "OMG. It's Shakespeare. The Shakespeare. William Shakespeare."

I couldn't believe it. Was this really happening?

"So we did travel back in time," she whispered. "To Shakespeare's time. That's hundreds of years ago."

I took a deep breath. "Now we know where we are. We just have to figure out why we're here. I mean, there are millions of kids on Earth. Why did we go back in time?"

"The flag has been changed to black," said Robert. "I do not know who raised the white flag."

Shakespeare sighed. "This wouldn't have happened at our theater."

Aubrey spoke quickly and in a quiet voice. "Now I remember. The color of the flags let people know if the upcoming performance was a tragedy, a comedy, or a history."

The door opened again. In walked another man.

"Thomas? I hope you bring good news," said Shakespeare. "Please tell me that we are to have a full house today."

Thomas lowered his eyes. "I do have bad news, William. It is the plague. It may have reappeared here in London."

"Is there word from Lord Mayor?" Robert asked.

Thomas nodded. "Word comes that two houses in Bristol have been boarded up and a red cross painted on their doors. And I am sorry to say that there are several more like them in Norwich."

Shakespeare rested his head in his hands. When he finally showed his face again, Robert spoke.

"That indeed might cause great alarm among the people throughout London if true. Norwich and Bristol are more than a day's journey from here. But enough travelers and pilgrims travelling to celebrate Christmas in days past have surely been through both towns. If so be true, the theaters will close once more."

Shakespeare stood and paced the room. "Let us hope and pray that news of the plague is only a rumor. For if the truth, the Curtain Theatre will be shuttered once more. If that is to happen, I am done with my time here in London. I shall move back to Stratford for the rest of my days."

Robert poured Shakespeare a drink from a pitcher and handed it to him. "Yes, the years from 1592 to 1594 when the theaters were closed were hard years. But now you sound defeated even before we know the truth. You cannot let this news get the best of you. Things are surely improving."

"I am sorry, but I am weary. In the four years since the theaters have reopened, I have dreaded the news of another plague. Just when we recovered and started to make money again, our theater was snatched away from us and we are forced to perform here."

Four years? I looked at Aubrey. She was as shocked as I was. We were talking to William Shakespeare. And it was 1598!

"The Curtain is not so bad," said Robert.

"To you, it is not, that is true. But my pockets are drained here. I do not make much money since I have no stake in the day's admissions. So, while I feel fortunate that the Curtain took us in, we must find a new theater that is ours alone."

"What if we don't find one?" asked Thomas.

"Then I shall take it as a sign that I am not meant to continue on this writing journey and return to my family in Stratford. It has been hard to leave my beautiful wife and children in the country. If I am making money, Anne then surely understands my need to be here. But if I cannot send her money, what is the sense of my staying?"

Both men looked uneasy.

Aubrey gasped. "No! You can't quit writing, Mr. Shakespeare. You have so many plays that you haven't written yet. Comedies, tragedies, histories. To stop writing now would mean that we'd never know your untold stories."

Shakespeare nodded slowly. "Do you know my work well?"

Aubrey's cheeks turned pink. "Everyone knows your work. Loves your work."

He smiled, then continued to talk about the plague. "The last plague killed many of my friends and some family members. When the order first came from the queen to shutter the theaters, I balked. But after their quick deaths, I understood the grave dangers that were to come our way. In the end, perhaps no shuttering was needed because almost everyone here in London left for the country or died trying to escape."

Thomas coughed. "A sad lesson we all learned was that there was no escaping the horrid disease. I am still fearful of it. Even today as my chest is heavy."

"You survived," I said. "And so did everyone in this room."

"Indeed we did," said Thomas. "But will good fortune be ours next time?"

Shakespeare let out a heavy sigh. "First I lost friends and family, then I lost my theater. 'Tis a hard life. We built that theater. Every piece of timber and joint was paid for not by the landlord but by us. For Allan Giles to tell us that since he owns the land so what stands upon it is his as well? A travesty!"

"Aye," said Thomas as he poured himself a drink.

"There is nothing we can do about it," said Shakespeare. "Giles becomes richer while we become poorer in spirit and pocket." He scooped his cup off the floor, set it on the table, and turned toward us. "I must focus now on the performance today. To thank you for the dresses and costumes, can I interest you in a gallery seat? I assure you it is much preferred to where the groundlings are."

I shot Aubrey a quick glance. "We'd be happy to watch from your seats."

"Thrilled," said Aubrey. "Honored."

"Very well," he said. "Robert will bring you to your seats after he helps Thomas into his costume. The play will begin in just a few moments' time."

After Shakespeare left, Robert picked up a dress from the pile on the workbench. "This belonged to a noblewoman from Kent. The fabric is beautiful and it is in fine condition."

"That would be our aunt," said Aubrey. She flashed me a huge smile.

The two men stood tall and bowed. "We didn't know. How can we thank you for all of your costumes?"

"If you may, my brother needs warmer clothes. And after he gets them, we would like to stay and watch Thomas prepare for the play. That is all the thanks we need."

While I wasn't happy to give up my shorts and sweatshirt, the clothes Robert found for me were at least clean and soft. Besides the robe, the clothes didn't look much different from the ones I had arrived in.

"I don't think I've ever worn velvet before," I said to Aubrey.

"Brown is definitely your color," she said.

Over the next few minutes, we learned that Thomas was playing Juliet. I thought it was strange that a man would play a woman's role and asked Aubrey about it.

"Acting wasn't considered appropriate for women," she explained. "So women's roles were played by men."

Thomas was getting dressed for his performance. "Oh, by thunder," Thomas said. "The fabric of this petticoat is so stiff, it will make me itch and cause me great discomfort."

"You have the same complaints each time you dress," said Robert as he picked up another garment. "Look here, my young friends. This is called a bodice.

I have to help young Thomas tie it in the back. And then we have the farthingale to add which will really make the skirt fill out."

The farthingale looked like three hula hoops of different sizes held together in the shape of a cone. When worn under a dress, it fills the skirt out and supports its shape.

I whispered to Aubrey, "We could use this stuff for Halloween!"

Thomas had the farthingale on. "Stay still for a second more. It is time for the dress," Robert said. He helped Thomas into an embroidered dress that looked like it was fit for a queen. There were dozens of buttons on the back that had to be fastened.

"And now the shoes," said Robert. "They will help Thomas walk in a ladylike and stately manner. It has taken him some time to get used to them."

"They hurt quite a bit at that," Thomas added. "Especially when I am walking with the added weight of this dress."

Thomas carefully lifted a wig off of a peg. "This is as heavy as the dress."

Robert spent a few minutes adjusting the wig to his head. "The next step is to add a small ruff around his neck and then the transformation is almost complete," Robert said.

Aubrey examined the ruff. "So that's what that thing is called. I've seen them in pictures before."

"You need makeup," said Aubrey. "Don't you?"

"We make it ourselves and it's a fine mixture," said Robert.

He grabbed a container and poured something into a pestle.

"Then I add a spot of ash, a green fig, and vinegar to it like this." He lowered the pestle for us to see. "I use the mortar to crush and mix it together. Once smooth, Thomas applies it himself."

Thomas dipped his fingers into the paste and rubbed it over his skin. It was a much lighter shade than his skin tone and looked like chalk.

After checking over Thomas from head to toe one last time, Robert smiled. "A fine and noble lady he is now, isn't he?" Then he focused on us. "Come with me. I shall show you to your seats."

As we walked out a different door that led directly to the stage, Robert stopped to help another actor adjust his costume so I asked Aubrey about the plague.

"So what do you know about it?"

Aubrey looked nervous. "It was also called the Black Death or bubonic plague. When we were here last year, my dad took us to the Museum Of London. We saw an exhibit. It was horrible, Mason. Scariest thing I ever learned about. Almost half of the population of London died. Half! People didn't know how it was spread or how to stop it."

"Are people still dying from it?" My heart raced. "What if we get it while we're here? Did they find a cure?"

Aubrey took a deep breath. "It happened a couple of times. The first time was in the 1300s. But the worst time was just before we got here. Rats and fleas spread it, and all of the filth in the streets didn't help. It slowly died out when people improved their hygiene and stopped dumping trash wherever they wanted. People learned to avoid crowded places, not to drink dirty water, and they eventually realized they had to burn the clothes and blankets of anyone infected."

I thought about the rats in the alley earlier and shuddered.

"People around here still have a long way to go before they figure out what the word clean means," she said.

I was worried. "We better figure out why we're here and leave as fast as we can. I don't want to get sick."

Aubrey agreed. She reached up under her dress and took out her hand sanitizer. She squeezed a little into her hands. Then she rubbed it all over her hands and arms before handing the bottle to me.

WHERE ART THOU ROMEO?

When Robert finished helping the man, he motioned for us to follow him up some steps.

"Here are your gallery seats. They cost two pennies per seat but you have the benefit of having a roof over your head in case of rain. Many feel it is well worth it." He pointed to a wooden bench and continued. "Now if you stood with the groundlings down in the yard, it would not be as enjoyable for a lady such as yourself." He pursed his lips. "Some of the men and women down there are the less desirables."

He scanned the area below and pointed to two men fighting. One was holding a dagger!

"I can see today's groundlings will not disappoint," he said as he turned to leave. "I do hope you enjoy the performance."

"Is that part of the show?" I asked. "Someone is going to get killed down there!"

Aubrey frowned. "Nope. I don't think so. This is a crazy time in history where men and women fought in public all the time about anything and everything. They drank a lot and that made the arguments last longer. Have you noticed that everyone seems to have a sword or a dagger?"

"It's kind of hard to miss," I said. "It looks like that's how they solved their problems."

I didn't want to see the outcome of the duel so I concentrated on looking at the rest of the theater. The first thing I noticed was that the stage jutted out into the yard where the groundlings stood.

The galleries were three stories tall and surrounded the stage and the yard. The whole place reminded me of a football stadium back in Texas. There were two thick pillars holding up the roof at the back of the stage. At the highest point, there was a roofed tower with green, red, and black flags.

A minute later, we wiggled over to the center of the bench to make room for three men who had entered the gallery.

"These seats are tiny," said Aubrey. "I feel cramped sitting here."

"Cozy," I said. "Just like the Austin, remember?"

"Yeah. How could I forget?"

The man next to us smiled and revealed black and rotted teeth. He smelled like he had been dipped in a sewer drain.

Aubrey covered her mouth and nose. "I think I'm gonna be sick. The smell is too much, Mason. The dirt. The germs." She pulled her feet up underneath her. "It's everywhere. I'm itchy just thinking about it." Her eyes darted all around the theater. "This would never pass health inspections back home."

"Try not to think of it," I said. "Concentrate on something that smells good."

She closed her eyes. "I smell the cinnamon sprinkles from my cookies."

"Good," I said. "And if you really think you're going to get sick, do me a favor?"

"What?" she whispered.

"Throw up on the other side of you."

She punched me in the arm.

"I'm starving," she said. "Aren't you?"

The man next to us heard. "I have an extra apple that I was going to throw at one of the actors." He held up a perfectly red, shiny, round apple. "But you can have it."

Aubrey looked disgusted by the man. "No, that's okay. Keep it." Then she added, "But thanks for asking."

He stood. "I insist."

Aubrey took a deep breath. "Well, I am sort of hungry." She stretched out her hand.

Right before he gave it to her, he took a bite out of it. As he pulled it away from his mouth, a string of saliva came with it.

Aubrey gagged.

I nudged her down the bench. "She's allergic to apples."

Once again, she pulled out her hand sanitizer and rubbed some all over her hands and arms. At this rate, she'd run out before the play started.

After a few minutes, she calmed down.

"This place, minus the dirt and scum of course, is amazing. It's almost exactly like the new Globe Theatre and in some ways not that different from the Austin when you think about it." She scanned the area above us. "There's another whole tier of seats up there, except the people up there look like royalty."

"I miss my family," she said. "And I can't believe that I'm saying this, but I wish we were back in Austin right now. Meeting Shakespeare and seeing the past is all pretty cool but I would feel so much better if I knew when we were going back home."

I said, "As soon as this play is over, we'll start to brainstorm ways we can get back home."

Aubrey nodded as she watched more people

trickle in. It wasn't long before the entire yard and galleries were filled.

"I wish the Austin could pack them in like this," she said. "Then no one would have to worry about it closing down."

Just then, a man dressed in a red vest with white and yellow striped sleeves appeared in the tower's window and blew a trumpet.

Aubrey clapped. "That's exactly what they did at the new Globe. It signals the start of the play."

But instead of quieting down, the people got noisier. Rowdier.

There was a lot of shouting and cursing. Men raised their mugs and drained them in seconds. A few women walked among the crowd selling apples, pears, and nuts. Every time a man got too close to one of the women, she'd punch him in the stomach. Most of the men would fall to the ground and stay there.

"I think they've had too much to drink," I said. "Either that or the women here are super strong."

"Oh, no," she said with a slight smile as she pointed down at the groundlings. "Get ready."

"For what?" I asked.

She squinted her eyes and covered her face for a second. "Anyone who drinks a lot has to use the bathroom, right?"

I laughed. "Yeah? So?"

She pointed to the back of the yard under the gallery. "They don't have bathrooms here so people go over there and, well, you know."

"Just like that?" I said. "In front of everyone?"

She shuddered. "Just like that. And they obviously don't wash their hands after they go either." Then her eyes bulged. "I bet a lot of people around here have worms."

"Whoa!" I said. "How gross is that?"

I was starting to realize why everything and everyone smelled so bad and why so many people died from the plague.

Before we had time to finish talking, the crowd

roared with laughter as a man in a red cap appeared on stage. He danced around in circles as he played a flute-like instrument. After several minutes, a few apples bounced onto the stage just missing him. The crowd roared again.

"He's the opening act," Aubrey said.

"He looks like Robert," I said. "With a beard."

"It could be," said Aubrey. "The actors and stage workers sometimes played several roles and had a couple of jobs."

The clown disappeared behind the curtain. The people sitting in the galleries settled down but many of the groundlings continued laughing and talking among themselves.

Finally, an actor dressed in a gray robe and black stockings and wearing a hat stepped forward from behind the curtain and spoke in a booming voice.

"Two households, both alike in dignity, In fair Verona, where we lay our scene . . ."

Then he gave an introduction to *Romeo and Juliet* and told us about the characters.

Aubrey sat on the edge of her seat as she watched the opening scene. "This is the most famous love story ever written. My mom says that some people consider it a comedy because of all the silly squabbling between Romeo and Juliet's families."

A sword fight erupted. The crowd cheered as if it were real.

"It looks so real, doesn't it?" she asked.

"What noise is this, give me my long sword, ho!" shouted an actor.

Even though they didn't use microphones and the crowd was noisy, I could hear every word. Each actor faced the crowd and spoke loud and clear. Everything looked so real that I forgot I was actually watching a play until Aubrey poked me.

"Look up there, Mason. Behind the stage. I bet that part of the gallery is going to be the balcony. The most famous scene in the play is coming up."

And a minute later, Thomas, dressed as Juliet, stepped onto the balcony.

"O Romeo, Romeo wherefore art thou Romeo?
Deny thy father and refuse thy name . . ."

I rolled my eyes. "Isn't it a little silly how fast they fell in love with each other?"

But Aubrey wasn't listening. Her eyes were glued to the balcony.

When it was over, Aubrey sat quietly for a minute. Then she wiped her eyes. "It was perfect," she said. "Just perfect. What did you think?"

"It was better than I thought. Different than I thought. A lot of the actors talked directly to us and explained what was happening. They don't do that at the Austin. And there really aren't many props besides their clothes. Did you notice that if they needed a prop like in the grand ball scene, the props were brought out on stage just until it was used and then whisked away? And what's up with no background scenery?"

"Because the words of the actors have to create the scenery in your head," said Aubrey. Then she cracked up. "At least that's what the tour guide said!"

As we got up to leave, Shakespeare came toward us. "Did *Romeo and Juliet* meet your expectations?"

"We loved it," said Aubrey. "It was an honor to see it. Mason memorized the part of Juliet. I was impressed. We wish we could repay your kindness."

His eyes sparkled. "Every word of Juliet? You did not tell me you saw the play before. I find this an interesting turn of events." He put his hand on my shoulder. "You can repay me. We need another actor for the role of Juliet for tomorrow's performance. All this talk of the plague returning has turned Thomas into a sick billy goat. He says he feels too ill to perform. And if you know every word as you say you do . . ."

Aubrey jumped in. "I'd love to do it! I won't let you down."

Shakespeare looked puzzled. "Surely you don't suggest that I have a woman on the stage, do you?"

Aubrey looked crushed but bounced back. "I knew you meant Mason. He'll do it, right Mason?"

"I will? No! I don't act," I said. "I can't."

Aubrey waved me away. "I can get Mason prepared for tomorrow. Promise. But under one condition."

"Speak your mind," said Shakespeare.

"If we have to travel home tonight it would be impossible to return in time for tomorrow's performance. Can we stay here for the night?"

Aubrey was a genius!

"In the tiring room," she said

"A lady such as yourself?" asked Shakespeare. "What would others think?"

She shrugged. "It will give me an opportunity to assess what is in your tiring room and consider what items my family can contribute in the future."

Once Shakespeare heard the promise of future gifts, he agreed. "Your wish is granted. And now I shall be in debt to you both."

When we got back to the tiring room, I flipped

out. "I'm not an actor. I'm not going to do it, Aubrey. No way. What were you thinking?"

She folded her arms and narrowed her eyes. "I was thinking that we are hundreds of years away from home. I was thinking that we have no idea how we're getting back home or if we'll make it back to Texas ever again. I was thinking that we needed a safe place to sleep. Stop acting like a baby." She tapped her foot. "Unless you want to sleep out there with the rats?"

Aubrey was right. If we wanted to stay safe tonight, I'd have to play Juliet tomorrow.

It was time to stop acting like a baby and start acting grateful.

A PLAGUE SCARE

Shakespeare soon came to the room with three men. By now, we realized they also used this room as an office. Shakespeare sat in a chair and sorted through a stack of large papers as they discussed the play.

As Aubrey and I shuffled through costumes, another man entered holding a large clay pot with a slit on top.

"Aye, Augustine," one of the men said. "How did we fare today? Is the box heavy?"

"I just retrieved it from the office. I shall let us all see right now." He lifted it above his head over the opposite table and dropped it. It smashed into pieces revealing hundreds of coins.

Shakespeare walked over and sifted through the

coins. "Aye, my colleagues. A good take for today's performance. *Romeo and Juliet* is surely a success."

Despite the money piled on the table, Shakespeare didn't seem as happy as the others. He looked over at us and his expression changed quickly. A smile came over his face as he motioned us over to him.

"My fellows," he said to the men as he placed his hands on our shoulders. "Forgive me for being somewhat rude but I want to introduce you to my young friends. This is Master Mason and Lady Aubrey. Their noble family has kindly donated several fine costumes to our troupe. They will be staying in our company for a short sabbatical."

The men stood.

Shakespeare then introduced each one of them. "My colleagues are part of our Lord Chamberlain's Men. May I present Richard Burbage, Cuthburt Burbage, John Heminge, and Augustine Phillips."

Each man gave us a slight nod and a welcoming word before sitting back down.

"Furthermore," Shakespeare said, "Master Mason will be a stand-in for Thomas tomorrow. We have no one else who is able to perform."

He turned toward me. "I trust you will do your best." Then he laughed. "And I trust your best will be better than I anticipate."

Aubrey patted me on the back. "Don't worry! Mason will be great. He's so good, you may want him to play Julius Caesar."

Shakespeare shot Aubrey a suspicious look. "Why do you speak as if you know what our next play could be?"

Aubrey's face turned red. She shrugged. After a second, he bit his lip and continued to speak.

"Come share some food with us. We are hungry and would be honored to dine with you."

Aubrey seemed nervous and pulled me aside. "I don't think this is a good idea. The place is probably going to be filthy. I can picture the rats and mice. And the plates? I can only imagine the grime."

My stomach growled. "I'm starving. We'll just be careful not to eat anything strange. Most of what the people ate at the play today wasn't anything that we wouldn't eat."

"It wasn't cleaned, though," Aubrey said. "Nothing was."

We followed Shakespeare and the other men out the door. Augustine turned and locked it with a huge key.

"Plenty of riffraff in the street at night," he said. "We don't want thieves making way with our costumes."

We walked across the square and followed a route down toward the river. The sun had set and a cool breeze was blowing in from the water.

"Ugh," Aubrey almost gagged. "That smell is worse than before!"

John laughed. "Aye, my young friends, the tide of the Thames is low now. Those muddy banks smell rotten, eh?"

"Why do they smell so bad?" I asked.

"An easy answer," said John. "Because most people empty their chamber pots and garbage into the river. It's also where many of the tanneries and butchers throw their waste. Everything here in the street washes down to the river when it rains."

Aubrey winced. I had to hold my breath. But the men didn't seem bothered by it.

We walked a few blocks down the narrow sidewalk. Although some shopkeepers were sweeping out their stores, most of the shops were boarded up for the evening. Small mountains of trash were piled up in the street and every once in a while, I'd see the shadow of a rat.

"Ah, here we are my friends," Augustine said. "A fine establishment awaits."

We stepped up to a brightly lit storefront. A sign above the window had a crest with a red lion and a knight on it. The smell from inside was a welcome change. I heard people laughing and talking inside.

"Welcome to the Sir George and Dragon Inn," Cuthbert said as he held the door for us.

We ducked into the smoky room. Although it was busy, there were plenty of open tables. The room had a beamed ceiling and the walls were made of wood and stone. A huge fire roared in the fireplace. When I looked down at the floor, I noticed it was covered with nutshells.

"Why do they throw everything on the floor?" asked Aubrey. "Don't they know about trash cans?"

A minute later, we were seated around a wooden table. Aubrey rubbed her finger along the edge and frowned.

"Sticky," she whispered. "Want some hand sanitizer?"

I shrugged. "This place seems okay."

Audrey grabbed my hands anyway and squirted a few drops into them. "Rub."

"Goodness, but my stomach is empty," Augustine said loudly.

"Aye, and thirsty too," John added.

A woman wearing a filthy apron rushed over to our table.

"A good evening," she said cheerfully. Then she noticed us. "And what can I get ya lads? A tankard of ale? Cider or mead?"

We didn't know what to say.

"Water?" asked Aubrey.

Shakespeare crinkled his nose. "Water is not an option in London. It is bad for your health and can carry a pestilence."

Richard answered for us. "Two tankards of apple cider for our young friends."

"Fine at that," the woman said. "And for supper, what might I bring you? We got some fine rabbit stew, boiled eel, or mutton. Unless you fancy a beef pie?"

Aubrey froze. I wasn't sure what to do either. What I wouldn't give for a burger and fries at Hut's back in Austin.

Each of the men ordered the mutton or rabbit stew. Aubrey snapped out of her trance and politely said, "We'll have the beef pie."

As we waited for our supper to arrive, the men talked about the weather.

"How lucky we are that the favorable climate has extended our run well past our usual closing times," said Shakespeare.

"When does the theater usually close?" I asked.

"November. A month ago," he answered. "But as the weather has been unusually mild and we are trying to recoup some past losses, we kept it open. It has worked well. With the warm weather, the people of London have continued to come."

"But alas, the winter beckons," said Cuthbert. "The daylight grows shorter and the air has grown colder. It will snow soon so we are closing the theater in just a few days' time."

"Agreed," said John. "We have been fortunate that the weather has been our friend."

"Why exactly are you in the Curtain Theatre?" I asked. "You mentioned you were kicked out of your theater. What was the name of it?"

Shakespeare and the men became agitated.

"It was simply called the Theatre," said Shakespeare. "We own the building. But we do not own the land on which it stands. The lease on the land expired. A man named Allan Giles owns that land. He admits freely that he has no love of the acting and presenting of plays. We suspect that he wants the building's timber. The timber is quite valuable. He has proposed that we pay him a preposterous amount of money to extend our lease. Even with our success, we cannot afford to stay there. This is his way of taking what is ours and making it his own. To gain from our loss. This puts me in a dark mood."

Then the conversation switched over to the absence of Thomas.

"Thomas left for a spell to travel to the countryside," said Augustine. "He complained of feeling ill and hoped to return to his home in the case a quick exit out of the city might be at hand."

"He seemed to be feeling fine before the performance today," I said. "Why would he leave so quickly?"

"Ah, rumors of the plague causes one to panic and for good reason lad," said Richard as he took a sip from his tankard. "As you know, a good part of the population in London died from the plague. You were in the county?"

"Yes," said Aubrey. "We were lucky not to have suffered loss. Right, Mason?"

I nodded and swallowed hard. "Does Thomas think he is sick?"

Richard sighed. "It was Robert's news that spooked him. He is always worried that he will grow delirious with fever. Every dot that appears on his body makes him fear that they will swell and turn into black boils. He remembers all too well that death comes quickly to those who show the signs."

Shakespeare looked sad. "We all worry that the plague will return. It is never far from our minds. It is not uncommon now for many people to believe that they have the plague, when they don't. Robert's news of houses being boarded up spooked him. Thomas may have been a bit under the weather but me thinks he is in good health. But the plague brings out such great fear that we could not stop him from leaving."

"Anyone seen with symptoms will be shut in their place of residence and not allowed outside," Cuthbert added. "But thankfully, God be willing, Robert's words seem now to be just a rumor and a fright. There have been a few bits of panic over the past few months, but no outbreaks. With winter arriving, the plague is usually kept away."

The men all sat in silence for a few moments. I could see they were thinking about the possibility of the plague actually returning.

Aubrey quickly put her hands under the table again. I knew she was loading up on hand sanitizer.

The woman brought over two loaves of brown bread and two large mugs of apple cider. Then came our food. Although it didn't look like anything I'd eat back home, I was so hungry I just shoved it in my mouth. Aubrey did the same.

When we finished, the men insisted on walking us back to the Curtain.

"It is for your own safety," said Shakespeare. "There are many rouges and thieves roaming about. Trust me."

"No, we'll be fine. We'd hate to make you leave here before you wish to," said Aubrey.

I held her back. "No way, Aubrey. We're not leaving without them. If we can't trust Shakespeare, who can we trust?"

When we got back to the tiring room, Shakespeare lit the fire and showed us the chamber pot under the table. "Till tomorrow," he said. "A good night's dream to you both."

"Ugh. I almost forgot that there aren't any bathrooms or running water here," Aubrey sighed. "I'm not very excited about using the chamber pot."

"Well, the other option is the privy outside," I said. "At least the pot is inside."

"Yeah, but I still have to go out in the morning and empty it," Aubrey said as she headed for the door. She wasn't out there for long.

"Disgusting," she announced as she came back inside. "It's just a hole in the ground, right out in the open! No seat or anything. And it's a good thing I had some tissues with me." She squirted hand sanitizer on her hands and vigorously rubbed it in.

"When we get back to Austin, I think I'll have a new appreciation for bathrooms," I added. "And water. And soap." Then I thought about dinner. "The food was pretty good. The beef pie was kind of spicy and tasted like something my mom might cook."

"I might look up the same type of recipe online when we get home," Aubrey added. "I can make a batch for the next rehearsal at the Austin."

Aubrey sat down. "I've been thinking and I believe I know why we're here. In every time travel book I've ever read, people are always sent back in time to make something right or to make sure someone makes the right choices in their life. Maybe we're here to help Shakespeare save his theater."

I was skeptical.

"It could be up to us to make sure he gets his theater back," she continued. "He can't quit writing. If he does, the world will never have heard of the Globe

Theatre. No one in the future will have heard of him. That means no *Romeo and Juliet*, no *Hamlet*, *Macbeth*, or *King Lear*. We can't let that happen. We just can't!"

"So what are we going to do about it?" I asked.

She shrugged. "I figured out why we're here, now you gotta figure out how to fix it."

"What if I can't?" I asked.

"Then we could be stuck here. Forever."

We both knew that we had to get home and the sooner the better. Being with Shakespeare was kind of cool, but London during this time was scary. The streets were crowded, smelly, and filthy. There were plenty of shady and dangerous people around and most frightening of all was the talk of the plague returning.

"First things first," I said. "I have to practice my part before tomorrow's show and then we can start to think of a plan to get back home."

"We're lucky that you know the lines already," Aubrey said.

There was no script to follow but I found a large roll of paper pinned to one of the doors with the stage directions and actors' lines on it. I studied it for at least an hour before I took a break.

"I'm glad I got to see Thomas play the part today," I said. "I just can't believe that I have to dress up as a girl. How embarrassing."

"I don't think anyone in the audience will tell any of your skateboarding friends," Aubrey said. "Just think, it's going to help us get back home. I think."

She yawned. "Traveling back in time sure does make a person sleepy."

There was no way we wanted to sleep on the floor. We pushed some chairs and benches together to make beds. We folded a few of the costumes to make pillows. It wasn't as comfortable as home, but at least we'd be able to get some rest.

The fireplace gave the tiring room a warm glow. I fell asleep thinking about the day. It was scary but amazing at the same time.

It seemed that only minutes had passed before we were awakened by the crow of a rooster. The sun was starting to rise. I stoked the fire but it had long gone out and the room had a chill in it.

"Rise and shine, Aubrey!"

She groaned. "Are you as stiff as I am?"

"A little bit," I said.

We had no idea what time it was but we knew it was early. Aubrey climbed up on the workbench to get a good look outside.

"I see a few carts and wagons being pushed along the street and some people are near the markets. They aren't open yet."

"Good. That will give us a chance to go to the privy without an audience." I said.

After a quick trip outside and generous applications of hand sanitizer we cleaned up the room.

"I wonder when Shakespeare will come back?" Aubrey said.

"The play won't be starting until this afternoon,"

I said as I walked over to where Thomas had left the costume, makeup, and wig for Juliet. I shook my head and laughed. "I guess that I should start getting dressed. Like the Boy Scouts motto says, be prepared."

"Don't worry, Mason. I'll help you. Especially with the makeup."

I picked up the bodice and petticoat and held them out for her to see. "Look at these. How can anyone move with all of this padding?"

Aubrey turned around and covered her eyes. "I won't peek. Promise."

I did my best to put them on. "This petticoat thing is kind of stiff," I said. "You can look now."

Aubrey giggled as she came over and helped me tighten the bodice and get into the farthingale.

It took what seemed like all morning to get ready When I was finally done, Aubrey bowed to me. "My Juliet awaits her Romeo."

"These slippers are tight," I said. "I'm going to get a blister."

"I'd be more worried about athlete's foot," she said. "But I guess it's better to get fungus between your toes then the plague, huh?"

I groaned. "I don't want either."

Aubrey mixed the ingredients for the makeup and used a brush to put it on my face.

"I think that we have your ultimate Halloween costume once and for all," she said as she dabbed red blush on my cheeks.

"No thanks! This whole experience here might be some kind of trick but if we get home fast, that will be the ultimate treat."

It was hard to move around in the dress and I wondered why women wore so many padded layers.

We heard the door unlock and Shakespeare walked in carrying a large loaf of brown bread and a jar of jelly. Two of the theater workers followed and immediately relit the fire.

"Ah, all is well I see," Shakespeare said with a smile. "And our Juliet is ready for today's performance. My thanks again to both of you. We will raise the flag and blow the trumpets on the early side of the afternoon this day. There is a chill in the air and the sunlight will be minimal."

He left us with the jelly and bread which we devoured in record time.

Over the next hour or so, I practiced my lines and read over the playbill posted on the wall. Soon the other actors, as well as Lord Chamberlain's Men, arrived.

"Good day, young friends," said John Heminge. "What a fine Juliet you have become Master Mason!"

The others quickly put on their costumes and practiced making jousting movements with their swords.

We heard a commotion in the yard as the crowd gathered.

Aubrey promised that she was going to be in the yard right by the left of the stage.

"Which of these guys is Romeo?" I asked. "He's

going to have to give me a kiss. If anyone finds out about this ..."

"Just close your eyes and it will be over fast," Aubrey said as she waved good-bye. "It's just a peck. Don't forget, I'll be in the yard, stage left. If you forget your lines look over at me." Then she smiled before the door closed behind her and said, "Break a leg!"

Almost at the same moment, the trumpets sounded and the actors shuffled out the door. Although I didn't recognize him at first wearing a white beard, green outfit and red cap, Augustine Phillips stepped over to me and winked.

"Have a good show, lad," he said as he stepped out through the door.

I heard the crowd laughing as he did his dance onstage.

As the prologue began, I started to sweat. I wasn't so sure I could go through with it. The actors had their swords drawn and one by one each came over and gave me a nod.

Richard Burbage came over. "I'm taking Romeo's part today mate. No worries, I'll give you a peck on the cheek."

I felt so relieved!

As the prologue ended, the play began. Soon after the sword fighting, it was my turn to make an appearance. I held my breath for a moment and walked through the door and onto the stage.

A few men in the crowd whistled and some laughed. Everyone was dancing since it was the scene with the costume ball. I looked into the crowd and saw Aubrey mouthing the words "Good Pilgrim."

I cleared my voice. Richard, as Romeo, stood at the front of the stage and took my hand. He spoke to the crowd and then it was my turn.

"Good Pilgrim . . ." my voice squeaked and the crowd laughed. I tried again.

"Good Pilgrim," I repeated.

"You do wrong your hand too much, Which mannerly devotion shows in this; For saints have

hands that pilgrims' hands do touch, And palm to palm is holy palmers' kiss."

Just as promised, Richard kissed me on the cheek. I stumbled through my lines a few times, but nobody seemed to notice. Aubrey coached me through it.

Even though it was cool outside, I was sweating under the costume and my makeup smudged a bit. I didn't know there was liquid in the vial of poison and some splashed on my face and made the crowd laugh.

Then, at the climax, I heard gasps in the crowd as I faked my death. The play ended with Augustine doing his clown dance again. I was relieved as I crumpled onto the bench back in the tiring room.

The others in the cast and even some of the workers and stagehands came in to congratulate me. When Aubrey saw me, she jumped up and down.

"Great job!" she said. "You're headed to Broadway!"

Broadway? I wanted to head back to Texas.

CHAPTER
7

A MASTER PLAN

I changed out of my costume and felt both relieved and excited. It wasn't long before Aubrey gave me some advice on things that she thought I could improve on next time.

"Maybe you could be your mom's understudy back at the Austin," she said.

"And kiss Paul?" I said. "I don't think so. I'll stick to my skateboard and dirt bike."

"I think I need some air," I said as I removed the caked-on makeup. "I really wish I had my skateboard here. Or my bike. Although I'm not sure I'd have a place to ride them around here."

"There's not much fresh air outside, at least not around this part of the city," said Aubrey. "Especially if the tide is out."

"Let's go anyway," I said. "It's gotten a little colder. Maybe we can check out London Bridge before we figure out what's supposed to happen next."

We walked back into the tiring room where Shakespeare and the other members of Lord Chamberlain's Men were meeting again. Shakespeare was the only one who wasn't seated. He looked tense and paced back and forth.

"The air has grown cold and I sense it will get harsh," John Heminge said.

"Aye, but the show did well on this day," Cuthbert Burbage added. "And look here, it's Master Mason. Dare I say that his fine substitute performance is to be credited with the take of the coin today!"

The men applauded as we passed by. Shakespeare gave us a nod and a smile but soon returned to looking worried.

"I feel that there is no alternative but to relinquish my shares and retire to Stratford to pursue another line of work. It is only a matter of days before Allan

Giles is to prove victorious on his attempt to close this theater down and consume its parts."

The room was crowded so we hurried outside. The sun had disappeared behind the clouds and a brisk breeze kicked up dirt and papers from the street.

"Did you hear what he said?" asked Aubrey.

"Yeah, I heard it loud and clear," I added. "He's going to give up writing. We have to think of a way to convince him not to and fast!"

The sidewalks were crowded so we took a chance and walked among the foot traffic and carts moving slowly in the street.

"It may be cooler out," said Aubrey. "But it still smells. Look at all this trash."

We moved to the center of the street. There were wagons and carts carrying sacks of wheat and flour, crates of pears, and another wagon carried a large barrel of wine.

"What are we going to do?" Aubrey asked. "Time is running out. Shakespeare sounded tired. There has to be something that we can do to convince him not to give up. If we don't, there won't be any *Hamlet*. Or *Othello*. No *Twelfth Night* or *As You Like It*." She kicked a pebble. "And forget about *The Tempest*."

A small commotion started behind us. Kids were laughing and yelling. I noticed that people on the sidewalk were pointing.

"Pardon! Please allow me passage!" yelled an older man behind us.

Aubrey and I jumped toward the side of the street and saw a man pulling a flat wagon. On top was a fancy-looking dollhouse. He steadied the cart as it came up next to us.

"What kind of dollhouse is that?" asked Aubrey.

The man smiled a toothless grin. "Thank ye for your kind words, but this is no house for dolls. It is a replica of one of our majesty's most favorite country estates. It will be presented to her court as a gift."

We moved out of his way as he carefully rolled his wagon past us.

"Wow, that was pretty cool," said Aubrey. "It must have taken a lot of time and skill to make that model."

I agreed. "It reminds me of last summer when they shut down the road in front of the Austin. Remember that huge flatbed truck that drove by with that old house on it? They moved it away from the creek and put it over on Lamar Boulevard and turned it into a museum."

"I remember," said Aubrey. "They just picked it up off of its foundation and moved it."

Then it hit me. "Aubrey! I think I figured out a way to solve Shakespeare's problems.

"Why can't Shakespeare move the Theatre somewhere else? It can be taken apart piece by piece! Then Lord Chamberlain's Men can move the pieces and rebuild the theater someplace else. Maybe they can take it across the river and rebuild it over there?"

"That's a great idea!" Aubrey said excitedly. "It won't cost them a lot of money because the timber is already theirs."

"Exactly," I said. "Let's get back to the tiring room and tell Shakespeare!"

Aubrey and I ran back toward the theater. Lord Chamberlain's Men were still seated around the table when we got there. But Shakespeare wasn't there.

"Excuse us, gentlemen," I said as I tried to catch my breath. "Where is Shakespeare?"

The four men looked at each other and drooped their shoulders.

Augustine's hands shook as he put his head down on the table.

Richard Burbage spoke up. "Aye, Master Mason. He is taking a last look at the stage and the galleries before leaving for Stratford. There is little we can do to convince him that all is not lost. But perhaps it might as well be . . ."

Aubrey and I ran to the backstage area. We found Shakespeare standing alone on the stage.

"Mr. Shakespeare," I said. "We have an idea that might help you save your theater!"

Shakespeare smiled wearily. "Ah, my young Master Mason. The game is lost. We can never pay Allan Giles even if we were to run our performances through the winter months. Alas it has grown colder outside and my heart and desire to carry on has also grown cold. I accept my defeat."

"But we think this plan will work," Aubrey said. "Mason thought of it. It's clever."

"Then tell me," he said, "but I cannot promise I will favor it."

"What if you moved the entire theater to another location? You would need to take it apart piece by piece, move it somewhere, and reassemble it timber by timber?"

Shakespeare paused for a moment and rubbed his chin slowly.

"Hmm," he said. "The oak timbers used in the main structure are attached by pegs and joints. But with a hearty group of men, they can be removed in short order."

His face brightened. "It would be a heist of epic proportions!" He rubbed his hands together. "Let me confer with my fellow men. If they agree with me that this is a splendid idea, then we will be back in our old home in just a few month's time."

When we went to meet the others, Shakespeare burst through the door and stood in a theatrical pose. In a loud, clear voice, he spoke.

"My dear fellows. When all looks lost and the victory seems distant, a chosen few will find a way to rise up and grab the means to succeed. Our two friends here, Master Mason and Lady Aubrey have given us an idea. A plan. They have planted the seeds that will grow into our finest hour."

The men looked confused.

"Well, what of this idea or plan, William? Do tell," Richard said excitedly.

Shakespeare described the plan to take apart the theater and move the timbers to another location.

"Richard, does your family own that land directly

across the Thames near London Bridge at Bankside?" Shakespeare asked.

"Aye, William, yes we do. It is prime land, close by the river. We had designs for a theater there."

"Well then, a theater will indeed rise there. Our Theater," Shakespeare said. "We will contact Peter Street, a dear friend and able carpenter who can assemble a group of men in haste. We will work under the cloak of darkness and rapidly spirit away the timbers."

"This sounds like a truly genius idea," John said, "But what of Allan Giles. Will he not find us out?"

Shakespeare was quiet for the next several minutes. Then, he laughed and cracked a cunning smile.

"Giles is on a holiday as we speak. Let me say that his being away is the greatest gift we could wish for and one that he will wish he had never received."

TIMBER!

Just a few hours later, the plan was in place. Shakespeare, Richard, Cuthbert, and John had arranged for twelve carpenters and apprentices to meet them at Bishop's Gate. From there, we all made our way to Shoreditch and the Theatre.

"This is happening fast," I said.

"They don't have much time," said Aubrey. "They want to take all the wood before that man comes back. Shakespeare hopes to have all the timber in just a few days. Isn't it exciting?"

It was exciting. When we got there, we could see that some of the men had gathered around a fire pit and were waiting for directions. The sun had set a few hours ago and it was very dark and cold. We heard dogs barking in the distance and the occasional sound of laughter and loud conversations in the houses and barns nearby.

Thomas had returned from his trip and was waiting for us at the Theatre. He brought two heavy cloaks that used to be costumes for us to wear against the chill.

"From *Henry V*," he said with a wink.

"Aye, are ye all gathered?" said one of the men as soon as everyone had arrived.

He had long hair, a thick pointed beard, and a mustache. He wore a tattered leather vest and tan pants with heavy boots.

Thomas pointed at him and whispered. "Lads, that there is the finest carpenter this side of the Thames. His name is Peter Street and Master Shakespeare and the Burbages put all of their trust in him and his men to get this job done fast and easy."

I crossed my fingers. "This has to work, Aubrey. I'm ready to go home."

She grabbed my hand and squeezed it. "Me, too."

Some of the men lit torches and started placing them across the road around the Theatre. In a few minutes, the corner near the road was lit up. We could see the old theater clearly now. The long shadows made by the torches made the whole place feel a little creepy.

Shakespeare held up some type of blueprints near the fire. Another man took a thick stick and set it on fire to serve as a light. Peter Street, Shakespeare, and another man huddled around it and examined it closely.

"My father purchased the property and built this theater some twenty years back," the man said.

I tugged on Thomas's sleeve. "Is that Cuthbert?"

"Yes," Thomas said. "The whole family is in the theater business. They built many of the theaters in and around Shoreditch and across the Thames in the city itself. They are looking at the old blueprints to see where to begin taking down the Theatre."

As men gathered for instructions, we could see

their breath as they spoke. One man came back out of the dark and threw some wood on the fire. This allowed us to see everyone's faces a bit more clearly.

Shakespeare and Peter Street nodded as they blew into their cupped hands.

Shakespeare stepped forward and said in a clear, strong voice. "Friends and colleagues, thank you for your skilled assistance in taking apart the theater that has given us some share of reward over the years and that brought us through the pestilence with a degree of profit.

"In these next few days, under the cover of darkness, we will pull it down piece by piece. The position of each timber will be recorded and then it will be sent down Curtain Road to Bishop's Gate. There, we shall store it in a warehouse in Bridewall. Upon further arrangements, each timber will be carried by ferry across the Thames to Bankside where the theater shall be reassembled. But for tonight, we shall make the journey with just one of the timbers.

The first one that falls. We shall travel to our new home and display it proudly to remind us of what will soon rise from the ground."

Peter Street spoke up. "There are hammers, ladders, and ropes in the wagons. We shall start right in the front. The joints of the timbers are connected with pegs."

He was handed a sample by one of his men.

"Aye, my friends, once we get the first section apart, the others should come down with ease. But do be careful. Do not work with too much haste. We shall disassemble this building with ease, but be quick to be careful and safe."

Everyone headed toward the carts for tools and supplies. Peter Street was giving directions to small groups before they got to work.

Shakespeare and Cuthbert came over to where we stood.

"Cuthbert, as you know, these two youngsters hatched our noble plan," said Shakespeare. "I do think with Godspeed they should be given a large share of credit."

"Aye," Cuthbert said bowing to us both. "It is a plan that will not be thwarted. I knew of the clause in the lease that my brother had found and I was pained to think of trying to gather the funds to keep the theater here. So when William told of your suggestion of taking what is rightfully ours piece by piece and rebuilding in Bankside, I knew it was what must be done. It's a brilliant idea and I thank you from all of us involved with Lord Chamberlain's Men."

Aubrey and I sat down by the fire and watched.

"With all of this racket and fires being lit, I can't believe that nobody has called the police," Aubrey said.

"This is a tough neighborhood. I guess pulling down a building in the middle of the night isn't much of a distraction around here," I said.

All of the workers were busy in and around the empty theater getting it ready to take it apart.

"This will be just like building a big model airplane," I said. "Shakespeare and his men have all of the pieces to assemble a new theater, and they have the blueprints as instructions."

We heard workers talking and even shouting instructions at one another. There were a lot of hammers banging and the sound of wooden joints being pried apart. Ropes were hoisted up on ladders and some were hauled up through the window.

Two more horse drawn wagons with trailers arrived. We could hear a great deal of commotion coming from inside the theater and then someone shouted, "All is ready! Clear away from below!"

Five of the men below hurried back toward us a safe distance away. Thomas and another man unhitched two horses and lured them over to the front of the theater where they attached two of the long ropes to their bridles. The horses were then led away until the ropes between them and the theater tightened.

"Watch what happens next," I said to Aubrey.

A few more workers also picked up a rope that was let down from the window, tied it to a piece of timber, and walked out towards where the horses were waiting. Peter Street walked up right next to us carrying a torch. He raised it high in the air and waved it back and forth. Just then we saw a torch appear near the roof of the theater on the left side. The man holding it waved it back and forth as well.

Peter said, "That there is the signal." Then he shouted, "On my count, one, two, three! Pull away!"

The horses were let go and they lurched forward. The two large men yanked as hard as they could and pulled on the ropes as they trudged backward. All of the sudden, there was a loud cracking sound as the timber was pulled from the building.

"It's happening," said Aubrey. "It's really happening."

Suddenly, the first section of the theater broke free. As it teetered, men on the inside of the building used

long poles to push it away from the main structure. It fell down with a crash and landed in a cloud of dust. The workers all let out a cheer. The men started climbing on the fallen section. They used hammers and crowbars to pry planks away from the timbers. Although there was still plenty of dust blowing around, we went over to get a better look.

Shakespeare and Peter Street were studying the blueprints. Another man came up to them with a bucket of some kind of white paint. In a few minutes, the first of the large pieces of timber was freed from the debris. After meeting with Shakespeare and Peter Street, the man with the paint walked over and painted a number and letter on the timber.

"Wow," I said to Aubrey. "This will be like building a giant model, they're labeling each timber and joint, so they can put it back together just like it was here."

Within minutes, the whole process started again. And the last step each time was the painted number and letter.

The man saw us watching. "When we put it back together, each piece will have its place and . . ."

"That place is the new theater," shouted Shakespeare.

"Long live the theater," shouted Thomas.

I watched as everyone worked together. It reminded me of all the cast and crew at the theater back home. Even the kids pitched in to help make each play a success. Then I thought about the slow sales. And Miss Lucy. And all the friends I made there. That's when I knew that I didn't want the Austin to close.

"Long live the theater," shouted Cuthbert.

I crossed my fingers and made a wish.

Long live the Austin.

A NEW BEGINNING

It took half the men to drag the beam down to the shoreline where a barge was docked. The barge was steadied against the dock as the beam was loaded and secured with leather straps.

"This is the first of many timbers that will find their way to the other side of the Thames," said the waterman. "No one can keep Lord Chamberlain's Men down for long."

"Aye," said Shakespeare. "Only a fool such as Allan Giles would try."

Once the beam was secure, the waterman gave the signal to board. The night was chilly. The tide must have been in because there wasn't much of a stench.

Aubrey's hand covered her nose as if she expected the river to smell as bad as the man in the theater.

"You can take your hand away from your nose," I said.

She slowly moved her hand and sniffed the air. "It still smells bad but it's better than I thought it would be." She scratched her arm. "I feel so itchy here."

The waterman and his mates pushed off and began rowing over to Bankside.

Aubrey and I stood quietly in the back of the boat.

"Our plan worked," I said. "In just a few months, the new theater will be built. You don't have to worry about the Globe anymore. It's going to become a reality."

"Technically, that's not true," she said. "There will be a building but it may not be called the Globe. Did you hear them talking about the names a few minutes ago? Shakespeare is thinking about naming it the Earth." She sighed. "One of the men said it should simply be called the Theatre like the last one. That can't happen, Mason. History says it's the Globe Theatre. We have to make sure that history is right."

Aubrey twisted her ponytail around her finger.

"I was thinking the same thing," I said. "If we were sent back here in time to make sure Shakespeare didn't give up writing and that the Globe would be built, then I'm sure we're going to have to suggest the name to him before . . ."

"Before we can go back to Austin?" said Aubrey. "I wish we could just tell him it's supposed to be called the Globe but we can't, can we?"

I felt a hand on my shoulder. It was Shakespeare.

"My young comrades. I cannot thank you both properly. When our plan succeeds—and Godspeed it shall—we will benefit from heavy pockets once more. The Curtain has been good to us but has not allowed us to share in admissions earnings. Such is the way of business I suppose. And although I knew the proceeds would not be ours, I cannot express how angry it makes me feel each day. Each performance of ours only makes the Curtain richer when it should be Lord Chamberlain's Men who get the bigger share."

He sat down on the beam and continued. "But I feel hopeful tonight. The stars in the sky have aligned to give us good fortune. Our troupe has been dealt some difficult hands. First the plague closed our doors and, most recently, we lost the lease to the land. It has saddened me and I questioned my future with pen and paper. But for the first time in a long time, I have hope that springs from this idea that you have enlightened us with. I am looking forward to starting anew over at Bankside."

"The theater will be way better than the last one," I said.

"Unless there's another plague," said Aubrey.

"Do not mention that horrid disease," said Shakespeare. "The mere mention will keep people away. It will push Thomas to the brink. I do not wish to shutter the doors of this theater even before they open."

"Well," said Aubrey, "the Curtain is a mess. The plague is spread by rats and fleas. You have to keep the place cleaner. That will help control the rats."

"God is in control of the rats," said Shakespeare looking amused at Aubrey.

"But you can control the trash," said Aubrey. "There is trash everywhere! It is piled behind people's homes and stores. And the river is a mess. There wouldn't be so many rats if people stopped throwing garbage just anywhere. You need trash cans. And, if everyone put their garbage in one place, you might not have rats all over."

"And if there are fewer rats," I said, "chances are people won't get as sick."

"And what's the deal with letting people relieve themselves wherever they want to?" asked Aubrey. "It's disgusting. I saw people doing that wherever they pleased at the Curtain. If you let them relieve themselves anywhere in the yard, people will step in it. Flies will land in it and then land on food. Then who eats the food and gets sick? That's how germs spread."

"People must relieve themselves," said Shakespeare. "It is unhealthy not to do so when necessary. Again, it is out of my control."

"Then control where it happens," Aubrey continued. "Make the new theater a cleaner, healthier place to visit. You could dig privies away from the theater building. Maybe even build a wall to hide them. More upper class people might visit the theater and spend money if it weren't so gross."

"Gross?" He looked puzzled. "What an interesting word."

"It means . . . yuck," I said.

That made Shakespeare laugh. "Yuck?" He stroked his beard once again. "Yes, I can understand what you say." He was quiet for a minute. "I suppose you are right. This is indeed something that I shall consider." He stood and looked out across the river.

"My new friends, you have given my weary mind much to think about. I shall go and share your thoughts with the others."

"Do you think he'll listen to you?" I said. "Think he gets it?"

Aubrey sighed. "The plague does come back and eventually everyone realizes that they need to clean up around here. But maybe, thanks to us, Lord Chamberlain's Men will escape the disease."

The ride across the Thames was quick. We docked and followed Shakespeare and Richard up the bank. The moon lit the way to the landing. Behind us, Peter Street and his workers wrapped leather straps and handles around the beam. They hoisted it and began following us through Bankside.

Many of the buildings were lit with candles and lamps and torches illuminated the pathways. Even though it was late, there were still a lot of people out moving through streets that were crowded with carts and wagons.

"It's a lot busier over here," said Aubrey. "Maybe this neighborhood will help the theater make more money."

Richard carried a rolled piece of paper in his hands. "I think that's a map Richard is carrying," I said. When he pointed over to an open lot near a wooden pier, Shakespeare smiled.

A minute later, we stood in the lot. A few workers had gone ahead of us and lit torches to light the area. As soon as the beam was lowered to the ground, Richard and Cuthbert began to map out the location where the theater's foundation would be dug.

All of Shakespeare's men gathered around him to discuss how the building materials would be transported and where they would be stored before construction could begin in the spring.

Aubrey and I stood by Shakespeare as Peter Street's workers removed the leather straps from the beam. They dug a hole in which to place the beam. Then, they hammered it into the ground. Finally, the beam was set.

"Let this be a symbol of what is to come," said Shakespeare. "This beam will be the first of many. It is here on this night to remind us of what we once thought was impossible, is possible once again. The Theatre will rise once again."

Everyone cheered.

Shakespeare lowered his voice. "As much as I feel promise and positive feelings for the future of this bold venture, we have not come upon a suitable name for the theater that will arise from this empty spot. Richard suggested that we simply call it the Theatre once again but I feel we must be bold and daring for competition among theaters is fierce."

Aubrey rubbed her temples. I could tell she was trying to think of a way to suggest the name for them. She usually solved things quickly, but I suddenly remembered something that I had learned in school when we studied Greek mythology. My favorite myth, *The Twelve Labors of Heracles*, popped into my head.

"Um, Mr. Shakespeare," I said. "You have looked as though you have had the weight of the world on your shoulders."

"I have been worried, yes," he said. "Any money that is drained from my pockets is drained from the mouths of my children. I want this plan to work."

"Do you remember the eleventh labor in *The Twelve Labors of Heracles*? Atlas had to hold up the world on his shoulders and Heracles stepped in to help him? When Atlas tried to trick Heracles into holding it for eternity, Heracles tricked him into taking it back while he gathered apples? Why not call the theater . . ."

"The Globe Theatre!" Aubrey said. "Because, as we all know, all the world is a stage."

Shakespeare straightened his shoulders and looked at Aubrey. "I have used that phrase before and have planned to pen it. How did you know?"

Aubrey smiled. "Lucky guess."

Shakespeare stood for a moment and scratched his beard before pacing a few steps back and forth then he smiled. "And we are all players." His smile grew wider. "Yes, the Globe Theatre! Yes by Jupiter's moon, the Globe Theatre. I think it is wonderful. All in favor, say aye!"

Shouts of "Aye!" echoed into the night.

"We will need to let the people know we are here," said Shakespeare. "If we build here upon this land, then you know more theaters will come. We must stand out in some way and let them know that this is no ordinary theater. This is the theater where Lord Chamberlain's Men will rule the day."

"Advertise," I said. "That's what you do to get people to your business."

"Yeah," said Aubrey. "Mason's right. The Globe Theatre is going to be awesome. Let every person in London know you're here."

"I like that idea," Shakespeare said. "Now, if only we had a plan in place."

"It's not hard," I said. "You fly flags to tell the people what kind of play is performing, don't you?"

The men nodded.

"Make a flag that says the Globe Theatre," I said.

Aubrey spoke. "The flag showing Heracles holding the Globe. Fly it at the very top of the flagpole. Everyone will notice it and word will spread."

"Clever!" said Shakespeare. "Bravo! Now let us go back across the river to celebrate."

As we all headed back to the barge, Aubrey walked slowly, letting the others move ahead. She motioned me over. "We did it, didn't we?" she whispered.

"I think so," I said. "But we're still here."

Shakespeare and his men were already on the barge when we got to the pier. I stepped onto the boat ahead of Aubrey.

"You're not leaving me behind are you?" she asked. "Isn't it supposed to be ladies before gentlemen?"

Shakespeare extended his hand to her. "Let me help you, as you have helped me." Aubrey smiled and then turned to get one last look at the beam.

"Good night, good night. Parting is such sweet sorrow, That I shall say good night till it be morrow."

As she reached over and took Shakespeare's hand, her dress caught on something sharp. As she fell forward, I grabbed her other hand to keep her from falling into the water.

Suddenly, there was a flash of light followed by several more flashes. And when I saw it, I knew that it was so bright that it was going to lead us straight back to Texas.

I hoped.

CHAPTER 10

HOME SWEET HOME

The flashing lights finally stopped but it took a few moments for my eyes to adjust. My stomach had the same feeling I got whenever I rode a roller coaster.

I looked around and felt relieved. There were no signs of the barge, the London Bridge, or the Thames River.

"Are you okay, Aubrey? Are you here?"

"I'm here, Mason! Over by the dresses. Are you all right?"

She stepped out from the costumes and adjusted her foggy glasses.

"My dress ripped," she said. "I can't wait to take it off and look like a regular kid in sixth grade again."

"Are we really back?" She sniffed the air.

"We're definitely back," I said. "Can't you tell by the smell of old building and new paint?"

Aubrey slowly scanned the room.

"What are you looking for?" I asked. "Garbage? Rats? Signs of the plague?"

She smiled. "I just want to be sure we're really back in Austin. At the Austin Community Theater."

I pointed to my old coffee maker and my dad's bike. "Same props," I said. "We're back where we belong, Aubrey. Finally."

Just then, the door opened and Paul walked in.

"Hey, Aubrey, can I have another cookie? I'll pick off the sprinkles. I'm so hungry, my stomach actually hurts. I bet you've never been that hungry before."

Aubrey and I looked at each other and burst out laughing.

She grabbed the tray. "Take a handful. But wash your hands first. There are a lot of germs around here."

Paul looked surprised. "Around here?" He shrugged. "I'll take my chances."

I was about to take a cookie myself but stopped. "Toss me your sanitizer, will you? I really need to wash my hands."

Aubrey tossed it over. "Keep it," she said. "I have a lot of them at my house and I plan on buying more."

I had a sudden urge for water. "I'm so thirsty," I said as I walked out the door and took a sip out of the fountain. It wasn't cold but it tasted great.

Aubrey followed and leaned against the wall. "I can't believe we went back to England in 1598 and not only met William Shakespeare, but made sure he kept writing. We made a difference. If it weren't for your idea, the Globe wouldn't have existed. Think about it. If there had never been a Globe Theatre, I would never have seen *Romeo and Juliet* last year. We wouldn't be here all summer watching these rehearsals."

"A chain reaction," I said. "Every action affects another action. Neat, huh?"

As cool as it was, I was thrilled to be back.

"I'm glad that I could see the past, but I don't think I would ever want to go back there," I said.

"Me neither," said Aubrey. "It was dangerous and gross. And very scary. People back then didn't know much about the connection between cleanliness and sickness, that's for sure."

We went to the stage where the cast was in the middle of rehearsals. Some of the actors were practicing their sword fighting. The stagehands were working on some of the scenery.

Aubrey and I stopped for a moment and watched.

"Lord Chamberlain's Men were better jousters," I said.

She agreed. "I kind of liked it without the scenery."

We walked up the aisle to the back of the theater. Both our moms were sitting in a row with one of the directors.

"We're not leaving yet, Mason," my mom said. "There's still a lot to do here."

"It's okay," I said. "I'm not in any hurry to leave."

My mom looked surprised. "What did you find in the room back there? Some magical prop that made you change your mind about this place?"

Aubrey laughed. "Nah. Just a magical dress, right Mason?"

Aubrey's mom grabbed her hand. "Good news! Miss Lucy said she just posted the sign-up sheet for the fall children's production. It's *Hansel and Gretel*. Auditions are in a few weeks."

"Oh great," Aubrey said. "I'll sign up right now. I really hope I get the part of Gretel."

"Maybe I'll audition for Hansel," I said.

My mom felt my forehead. "Now I'm convinced that something magical happened back there."

Aubrey leaned on the row of seats. "So have ticket sales been getting any better?'

The director shrugged. "We don't know the numbers yet."

"Maybe we should consider advertising out in the community," I said. "You know, at the senior center in town and the libraries and schools. Even Shakespeare advertised his plays at the Globe Theatre."

"We should fly a flag out front by the road advertising the theater and maybe we should get some of the volunteers to clean up some of the bushes and trees and plant some flowers," said Aubrey.

"Sounds like a plan," said my mom.

Just then, Paul staggered over to us. "I'm not feeling so good."

"Hope it's not the plague," I said.

Aubrey laughed.

"It's not funny," said Paul. "My stomach really hurts. I think I need to go home. Can someone stand in for me today?"

Aubrey got excited. "Mason's a great actor. He'd be perfect for Romeo. He knows all the words."

"I think you should do it, Aubrey. "You know the words, too," I said.

"But she's a girl," said Paul, holding his stomach. "She can't play a boy's part."

Aubrey stood. "Sure I can. If boys had to play all the girls' parts back in Shakespeare's time, then I can play a boy during rehearsal today."

For the rest of the afternoon, I sat in the front row and fed Aubrey the few lines she had trouble remembering.

"Thanks, Mason," she said.

"No problem," I said. "You know what Shakespeare says, don't you?

She laughed. "All's well that ends well!"